Wild Dog in the City

Written and illustrated by Karen Romano Young

Collins

2

Many dogs live in cities,
but we don't see
all of them.

3

It's late at night in a big city.
Pet dogs sleep inside on soft
beds or warm floors.

4

5

Outside, a wild
dog called
a coyote wakes up.
Coyotes live in cities all
over **North America**.

6

Once, coyotes only lived
in the countryside.

7

Pet dogs and coyotes are similar,
but they aren't the same.

Coyotes have lower elbows.

coyote

Dogs have deeper chests.

domestic (pet) dog

Coyotes also look like other dogs.

coyote

wolf

fox

dingo

jackal

In the country, coyotes leave their **dens** to hunt in the daytime.

City coyotes sleep during the day
and go out hunting at night,
when people and pets are inside.

13

Coyotes are good for the city
because they catch rats and mice.

15

Coyotes are shy. Most people and pets will never see a coyote. But if pet food is left outside, a coyote may smell it and come near.

A lone howl – or a **chorus** of howls – is
a clue that coyotes are nearby.

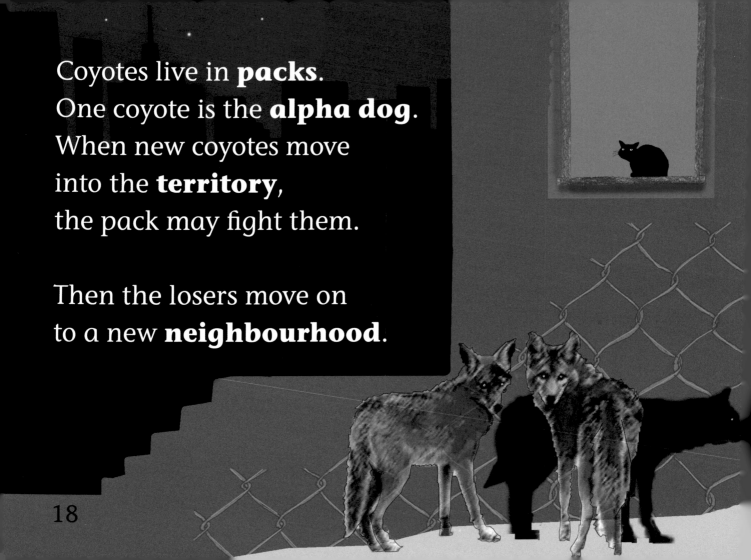

Coyotes live in **packs**.
One coyote is the **alpha dog**.
When new coyotes move
into the **territory**,
the pack may fight them.

Then the losers move on
to a new **neighbourhood**.

18

Right outside people's houses, coyotes keep their pups safe and well-fed.

Glossary

alpha dog	the leader of a pack of dogs
chorus	a sound made by a group of animals all together
dens	homes where wild animals live
domestic	tame, like a pet
neighbourhood	an area in a city or a town
North America	one of Earth's seven continents
packs	groups of dogs
territory	an area lived in by an animal or a group of animals

How do coyotes survive?

stay awake at night

defend territory

catch rats

feed pups

23

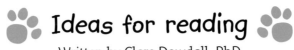

Ideas for reading

Written by Clare Dowdall, PhD
Lecturer and Primary Literacy Consultant

Learning objectives: linking what they read or hear read to their own experiences; making inferences on the basis of what is being said and done; giving well-structured descriptions and explanations

Curriculum links: Geography, Science

Interest words: alpha dog, coyote, chorus, dens, domestic, neighbourhood, North America, pack, territory

Word count: 206

Resources: paper and pencils; internet

Getting started

This book can be read over two or more reading sessions.

- Look at the front and back covers. Read the title and the blurb aloud. Ask children if they've ever seen a wild dog in a city, or describe a time when you've seen a wild dog.

- Lead a brief discussion about other wild dogs that the children know and have experience of (wolves, foxes).

- Look at the word *coyote*. Help children to say and read it. Notice the unusual pronunciation at the end of the word. Check that children understand that a coyote is a wild dog that now lives in cities in parts of North America.

Reading and responding:

- Walk through the book together picking out some of the interest words in bold print that the children may struggle to read independently. Model how to read these words and explain their meanings using the glossary.